I try to dig but the ground's too hard.

"It's no use, Grandpa. Everything's dead!"

He chuckles and his eyes are full of summer.

"It's only sleeping, Billy. Come and see!"

One slice of his spade and the soil turns inside out. Beetles, bugs and wriggling worms are busy breaking up the earth.

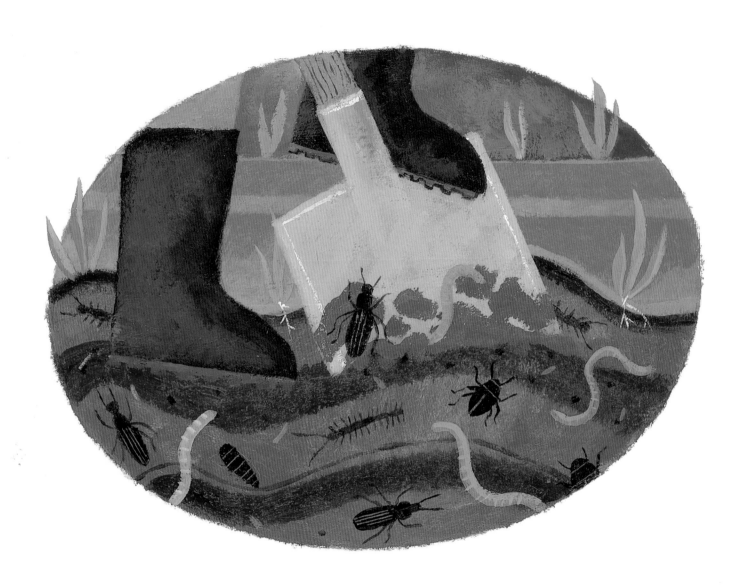

"Look how hard they work," says Grandpa. "Shall we help them?"

So we dig and dig.
All that digging makes my tummy rumble.
Grandpa says the soil is hungry too,
waking after such a long sleep.
"We need to feed it
or nothing will grow."

All year long, he's cooked a steaming compost heap.
Nothing is wasted. Vegetable peelings, lawn cuttings,
every fallen leaf. And now it's rich and dark and sweet
and ready to spread on our vegetable beds.
And then we wait.
It's hard to wait.

It's warmer now and lighter.

Leaves uncrumple, soft as silk, on waking trees.

Grandpa crumbles earth like chocolate cake.

"Ready, Billy? It's planting time."

We comb the soil smooth with our rakes and mark out lines with sticks and string. Peas and beans and pumpkin seeds need tucking in with careful fingers.

We sow carrot seeds in tidy rows. But I like scattering lettuce seeds into the breeze. Grandpa says they'll grow wherever they fall.

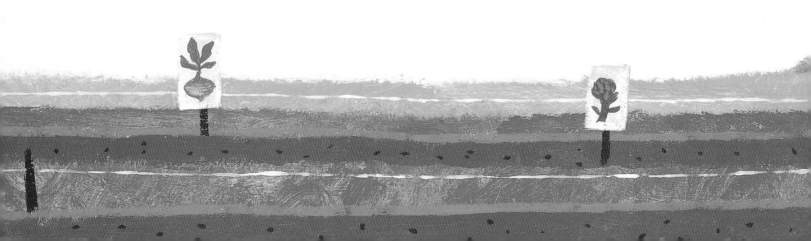

Grandpa has sprouted trays of potatoes.

We bury them and pat the soil around.

And then we wait.

It's hard to wait.

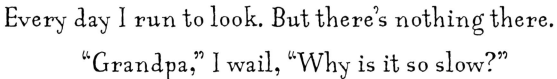

Every day I run to look. But there's nothing there.
"Grandpa," I wail, "Why is it so slow?"
"Patience, Billy," Grandpa smiles.
"Good things take time. But just
this once I'll let you peep."

A tepee marks the beans we buried weeks before. In
I dig, finger and thumb. A gentle tug and up one comes,
complete with brand-new baby roots. And look! Another
shoot is reaching up towards the light.

"There," says Grandpa. "Not long now!"

But it's still hard to wait!

Grandpa gives me jobs to pass the time.

Here, with my watering can, I'm rain-maker, cloud-shaker,
sprinkling rainbows on thirsty soil.

And now, as if by magic, spring bursts in and
everything grows.

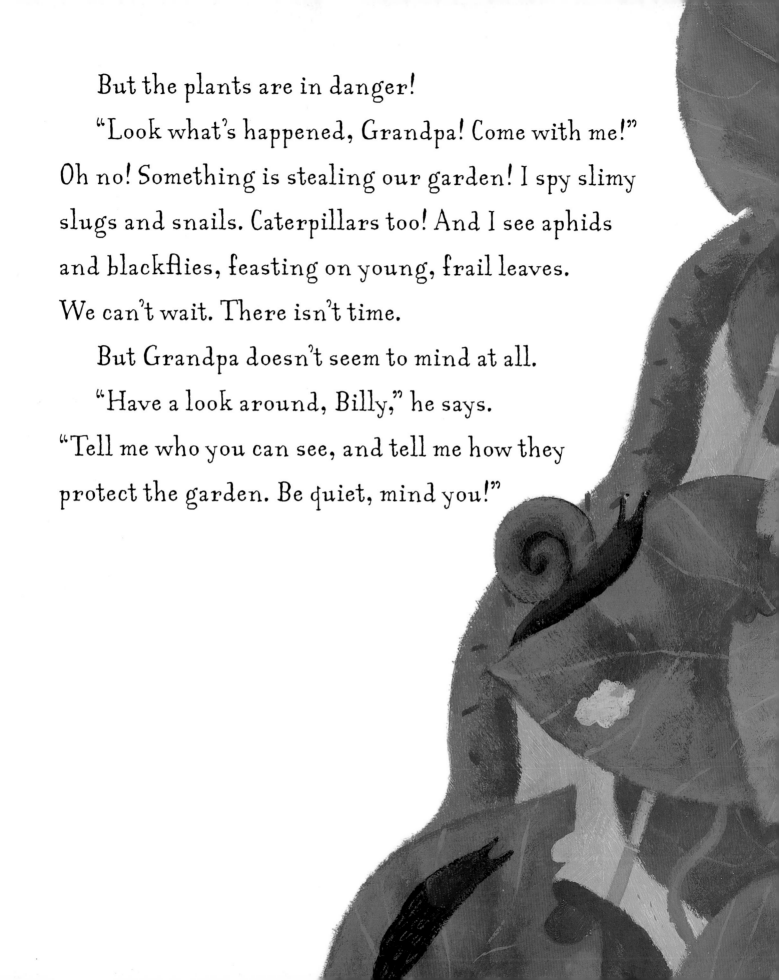

But the plants are in danger!

"Look what's happened, Grandpa! Come with me!"
Oh no! Something is stealing our garden! I spy slimy
slugs and snails. Caterpillars too! And I see aphids
and blackflies, feasting on young, frail leaves.
We can't wait. There isn't time.

But Grandpa doesn't seem to mind at all.

"Have a look around, Billy," he says.
"Tell me who you can see, and tell me how they
protect the garden. Be quiet, mind you!"

Very quietly, I start exploring. I find hungry frogs and snuffling hedgehogs.

There are lazy ladybugs and gauzy hoverflies.

And I see busy, bright-eyed birds fly down from the trees, searching for supper.

"They're the best friends we could have," says Grandpa. He's right! Our friends help keep those bugs at bay. And Grandpa knows a trick or two.

Everything's growing now in the summer sun, scrambling higher, squabbling for space.

Grandpa shows me how to pull out weaker plants and greedy weeds. We squeeze some room for baby plants — tomatoes, cucumbers and strawberries — grown in Grandpa's greenhouse.

At last it's harvest time! There's so much to do.
We dig and pick.
In no time at all my basket fills and my
mouth blooms bright with strawberry juice.

But when I pop a pod of peas I find that caterpillars have gotten there before me. "One for the compost," Grandpa says. "We have plenty more."

Grandpa leaves some peas and beans unpicked. The pods bake in the late summer sun until they crackle and split their seams.

Together we scoop the insides into paper bags. "These are next year's crop," he says. "I always grow a few more than I need."

The sun sinks, tender as the ripest peach.
We light a fire, Grandpa and me, roasting
potatoes and toasting our toes. Grandpa sips from
his flask of tea and I try to swallow my yawns.
Autumn is sending the soil to sleep and
it won't be long before winter's here.
But spring will follow and we'll be there,
Grandpa and me, to welcome it again.
And I can't wait!

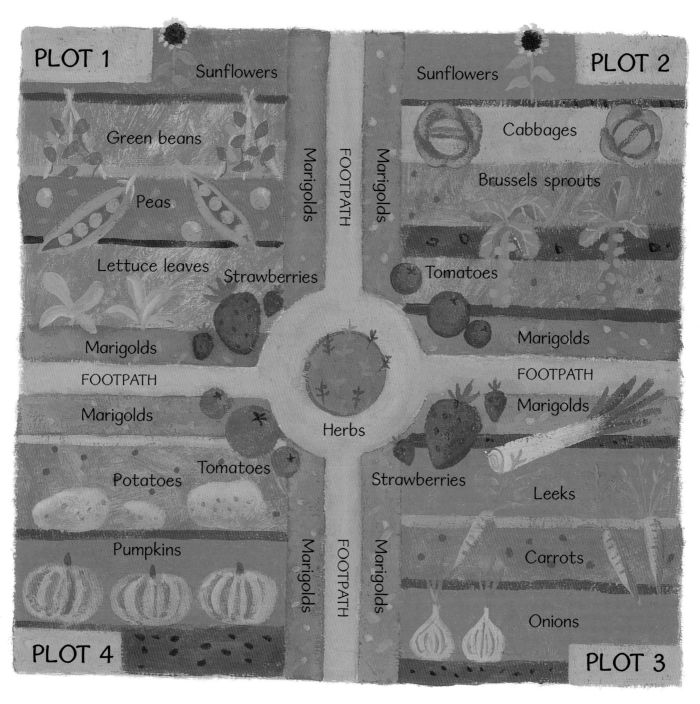

PLOT 1

Sunflowers

Green beans

Peas

Lettuce leaves

Strawberries

Marigolds

FOOTPATH

Marigolds

Tomatoes

Potatoes

Pumpkins

PLOT 4

PLOT 2

Sunflowers

Cabbages

Brussels sprouts

Tomatoes

Marigolds

FOOTPATH

Marigolds

Strawberries

Leeks

Carrots

Onions

PLOT 3

Herbs

Marigolds

FOOTPATH

Marigolds

PLOT 1

Sunflowers

Green beans

Peas

Lettuce leaves

PLOT 2

Sunflowers

Cabbages

Brussels sprouts

PLOT 3

Leeks

Carrots

Onions

PLOT 4

Potatoes

Pumpkins

FOOTPATHS

Marigolds

POTS

Strawberries

Tomatoes

Planning your Vegetable Patch

PLOT 1

Green beans and peas are also known as legumes.

They like to climb up bamboo canes or netting.

PLOT 2

Cabbages and brussels sprouts are also called brassicas.

Adding lime to the soil before planting helps them grow.

PLOT 3

Leeks, carrots and onions like to grow in finely raked soil.

The smell of onions is believed to protect carrots from carrot flies.

PLOT 4

Potatoes and pumpkins are easy to grow and can be stored to provide food for the winter months.

POTS: Herbs, strawberries and tomatoes grow well in pots.

CROP ROTATION

Plan your vegetable garden in different plots and rotate the plants each year. This practice — crop rotation — keeps your plants healthy by breaking the life cycle of pests, helping prevent disease, and keeping the soil fertile (full of nutrients) and easy to work with. Plants with deep roots help break up the soil. Some plants — raspberries, bushy herbs and apple trees — will be happy growing in the same place every year. Change the soil in the pots each time you replant them.

Grandpa's Winter

Grandpa spends the coldest months getting his vegetable patch ready for spring and planning all the good things he wants to grow. There are still a few vegetables in his garden — winter cabbages and leeks and brussels sprouts — and the canes from last autumn's raspberries are waiting until late winter to be cut back. He digs the beds and feeds the soil with compost and manure.

As spring creeps closer, Grandpa likes to sow some seeds inside his greenhouse where it's warm. Soon there are tiny seedlings nestling in trays. When the warmer weather comes they'll be strong enough to live outside. He stores the potatoes in dark places but puts the ones he is going to plant in the light to sprout.

Things to do in Winter

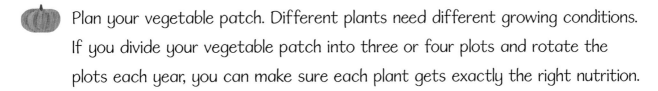

Plan your vegetable patch. Different plants need different growing conditions. If you divide your vegetable patch into three or four plots and rotate the plots each year, you can make sure each plant gets exactly the right nutrition.

Dig well-rotted farmyard manure or compost into plots 1 and 4 of your vegetable garden so that next year's legumes, potatoes and pumpkins get all the nutrients they need from the soil. Digging your vegetable plot over the winter also exposes the ground to frost, which helps break the soil down and improves its structure. When the earth becomes warmer you can dig out stones and weeds.

In late winter sow some seeds — like leeks, onions, tomatoes and parsnips — indoors, ready for planting out later in the year. Don't worry if you haven't got a greenhouse. A warm window sill works well. Special mini greenhouses called propagators also keep baby plants happy. Sprinkle seeds directly and evenly into shallow trays of damp seed compost. Cover with a thin layer of soil and make sure you label each tray so you know what you've planted!

Get a head start with your potatoes by putting seed potatoes in trays — old egg cartons work well. Leave them in a dry, light place until they sprout.

Grandpa's Spring

As soon as it is warm enough, Grandpa begins to plant seeds outside. He rests onions in rows and buries potatoes in trenches. He takes his seedlings outside — during the day only — to get them used to the weather until they are big enough to plant out. They don't like cold winds and late frosts! He welcomes friendly insects by growing sunflowers and marigolds and sweet-smelling herbs in among his vegetables. They're good to look at too!

Plants to grow directly outside in spring include peas and beans, sweetcorn, carrots, beets, pumpkins and squash. Although it is warmer, some more delicate seedlings, like cucumbers and peppers, still start life in Grandpa's greenhouse.

Things to do in Spring

Plant your potatoes outside in trenches about 30 inches apart with 10–15 inches between each potato. As soon as leaves start growing through the soil, cover the plants with earth from either side of your trench so you make a long ridge. This stops sunlight from turning the baby potatoes green and making them bad to eat. You can also grow potatoes in pots.

Delicate seedlings grown in trays indoors will need more room to grow. Carefully replant them into bigger pots of fresh compost. You can use an old dinner fork to ease underneath their roots; hold them gently by their leaves and not their stalks. As soon as the days get warmer, you can bring your plants outside — a little longer each day — to get them used to being outdoors.

Plant beans and peas directly into the soil — these are actually big seeds. If you soak them in water for a few hours, they'll grow more quickly. They'll need something to climb up, so first of all you can make tepees for beans (plant 8 inches apart) and push twiggy branches into the ground for peas (leave about 2 inches between each pea). If you plant pumpkins, remember that they like lots of room to spread.

Sow carrot seeds thinly in rows between your onions to discourage nasty bugs. Cover your sowings with old net curtains or chicken wire to keep pests away!

Grandpa's Summer

Grandpa is always busy now, weeding and watering from dawn to dusk, but he still finds time to enjoy his lovely garden. Greedy plants like tomatoes like to be fed with seaweed soup. As the days get longer and warmer, Grandpa can harvest all the tasty things he's grown. There's so much to pick he can hardly keep up. Soft fruit and vegetables are best eaten straight away, but he freezes or preserves anything extra.

Other crops can be stored. Grandpa puts his potatoes in big paper sacks and lays carrots and other roots in wooden boxes filled with sand. He leaves onions to dry in the sun for a few days before plaiting their leaves together and hanging them until he needs them. There's always plenty to share with friends and family.

Things to do in Summer

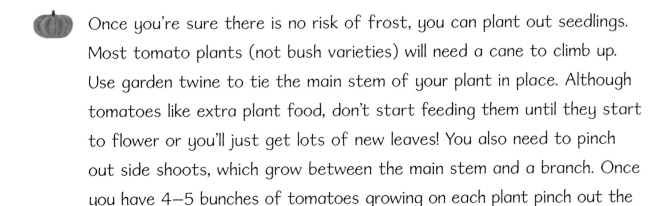 Once you're sure there is no risk of frost, you can plant out seedlings. Most tomato plants (not bush varieties) will need a cane to climb up. Use garden twine to tie the main stem of your plant in place. Although tomatoes like extra plant food, don't start feeding them until they start to flower or you'll just get lots of new leaves! You also need to pinch out side shoots, which grow between the main stem and a branch. Once you have 4–5 bunches of tomatoes growing on each plant pinch out the top to help the fruits grow bigger. You can grow delicious tumbling cherry tomatoes in hanging baskets if you don't have much space!

Thin out rows of new seedlings so that the ones that are left have more room to grow. Beets, lettuce and spinach seedlings are tasty in a salad so don't waste them!

Weeds grow well in the summer too! Get rid of them — weed often a little at a time and don't leave any roots — so that they don't steal moisture or nutrients from your vegetables. Gardeners use a tool called a hoe to weed between rows of vegetables but you can also weed by hand. Make sure that weeds like dandelions don't get big enough to scatter their seeds.

Pick peas and beans regularly and your plants will grow more for you. Put empty pods on the compost heap.

Grandpa's Autumn

The mornings and evenings are chilly now. But Grandpa's vegetable patch is still a busy place and pumpkins glow like lanterns on their vines. As plants die back he feeds them to the compost heap, saving seeds to dry and grow next year. Seeds from crops like tomatoes and pumpkins need to be carefully washed and dried so that they won't rot. He wraps apples in newspaper and rests them in trays so they won't rub against each other and spoil.

Grandpa cleans and oils his rake, spade and fork and hangs them in the shed, but he never tidies up too much in the garden! Animals need safe places to hide during the colder parts of the year and hungry birds find a feast in dead sunflower heads.

Things to do in Autumn

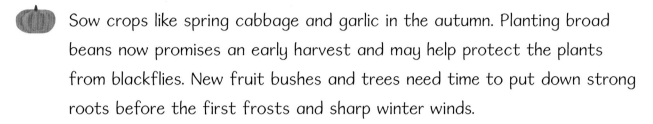 Sow crops like spring cabbage and garlic in the autumn. Planting broad beans now promises an early harvest and may help protect the plants from blackflies. New fruit bushes and trees need time to put down strong roots before the first frosts and sharp winter winds.

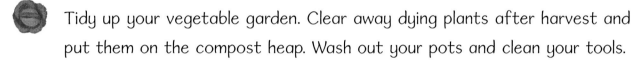 Tidy up your vegetable garden. Clear away dying plants after harvest and put them on the compost heap. Wash out your pots and clean your tools.

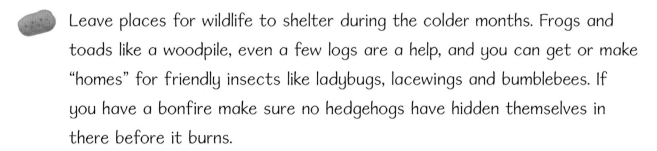 Leave places for wildlife to shelter during the colder months. Frogs and toads like a woodpile, even a few logs are a help, and you can get or make "homes" for friendly insects like ladybugs, lacewings and bumblebees. If you have a bonfire make sure no hedgehogs have hidden themselves in there before it burns.

Save some seeds for next year's garden! Peas and beans work well. Wait until pods are brown and dry and you can hear the seeds rattling about inside. If you tie a paper bag over the pod you'll save everything inside if the pod splits. Seeds from ripe tomatoes must be carefully washed — you need to get rid of all the soft jelly around each pip — then dried quickly. Store your seeds in airtight jars in a cold, dry place and make sure you label each container clearly.

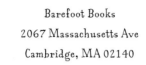

Barefoot Books
2067 Massachusetts Ave
Cambridge, MA 02140

Text copyright © 2012 by Stella Fry
Illustrations copyright © 2012 by Sheila Moxley
Cover typography by Owen Davey
The moral rights of Stella Fry and Sheila Moxley have been asserted

First published in the United States of America by Barefoot Books, Inc. in 2012
The paperback edition first published 2012

Graphic design by Louise Millar, London
Reproduction by B & P International, Hong Kong
Printed in China on 100% acid-free paper
This book was typeset in Aunt Mildred and Neu Phollick Alpha
The illustrations were prepared in oil pastels

Hardback ISBN: 978-1-84686-053-9
Paperback ISBN: 978-1-84686-809-2

Library of Congress Cataloging-in-Publication Data
is available under LCCN 2006026852

5 7 9 8 6 4